Taxi Driver!
Dashing Around New York City

Written by Robyn Brode

Illustrated by Paul Hayes

BARRON'S

This book is dedicated to the memory of the
World Trade Center's Twin Towers.

First edition for the United States and Canada published exclusively by
Barron's Educational Series, Inc. in 2002

Created and produced by Orange Avenue Publishing, Inc., San Francisco
© 2002 Orange Avenue Publishing, Inc.
Illustrations © 2002 Paul Hayes

All inquiries should be addressed to:
Barron's Educational Series, Inc.
250 Wireless Boulevard
Hauppauge, NY 11788
http://www.barronseduc.com

International Standard Book No. 0-7641-2150-2

Library of Congress Catalog Card No. 2001097894

Printed in Singapore
9 8 7 6 5 4 3 2 1

Taxi Driver!
Dashing Around New York City

More people live in New York City than any other city in the United States.

New York City is located in the state of New York.

United States

New York

My mother drives a bright yellow taxicab all over New York City. She is called a cabbie.

Sometimes when I don't have school, I get to go with her as she picks up and takes people all around town.

We get up early and get ready
to go. I like to watch the lights
go on in Manhattan as it begins
to wake up in the morning.

We walk to a garage where lots of taxicabs are parked. Mom finds the cab she drives.

She makes sure the gas tank is full and checks the meter. Then off we go!

Lots of people are waiting for a cab this morning. Most of them are going to work.

DID YOU KNOW?

In New York City, you can only hail cabs that are painted yellow.

One woman who hails our cab is going shopping on Park Avenue. Mom turns on the meter.

Next, we pick up a family of tourists and take them to a ferry in one of New York City's harbors.

The ferry will take them
to the island where the
Statue of Liberty is located.

Our next passenger wants to go
to the United Nations building.

After that, someone wants
to go to the famous Metropolitan
Museum of Art.

DID YOU KNOW?

Streetstands sell many kinds of food — popsicles, pretzels, and knishes, to name a few.

From there, we cut across town by driving through Central Park. We see lots of people picnicking on the grass.

We'll have our picnic in the taxi.
We stop to buy food and drinks
from a streetstand.

After lunch, our next stop is the New York City Library. Lots of cabs means lots of traffic!

The rest of the day people hail
us and we take them where
they want to go. In Chinatown,
I buy fruit for a snack.

At the end of the work day, lots of people hurry to catch a train from Grand Central Station to their homes outside the city.

Many others wait in line for buses and ferries. Still others we drive all the way home.

It's been a long, busy day. We're ready to go home. Mom turns off the meter and heads toward the parking garage.

On the way, I think of the people we have met and the places we have seen in New York City.

It's getting dark when Mom drives the taxi into the garage and parks it.

On our way home, we walk through Times Square. I like looking at all the lights!

Tonight, fast asleep, I'll dream I'm dashing around New York City in my own taxicab.

And if I can't sleep, I'll count taxis, not sheep!

MANHATTAN

When people say New York City, they usually mean Manhattan. Its nickname is the "Big Apple."

Manhattan is often considered the center of business and trade, finance, and culture in the United States.

Most of Manhattan is an island that is $12\frac{1}{2}$ miles/20 kilometers long by $2\frac{1}{2}$ miles/4 kilometers wide.

More than 2 million people live in this small area, and a lot more work there.

During the week, people who don't live in Manhattan commute to work. They travel from other towns in New York, and even from neighboring states.

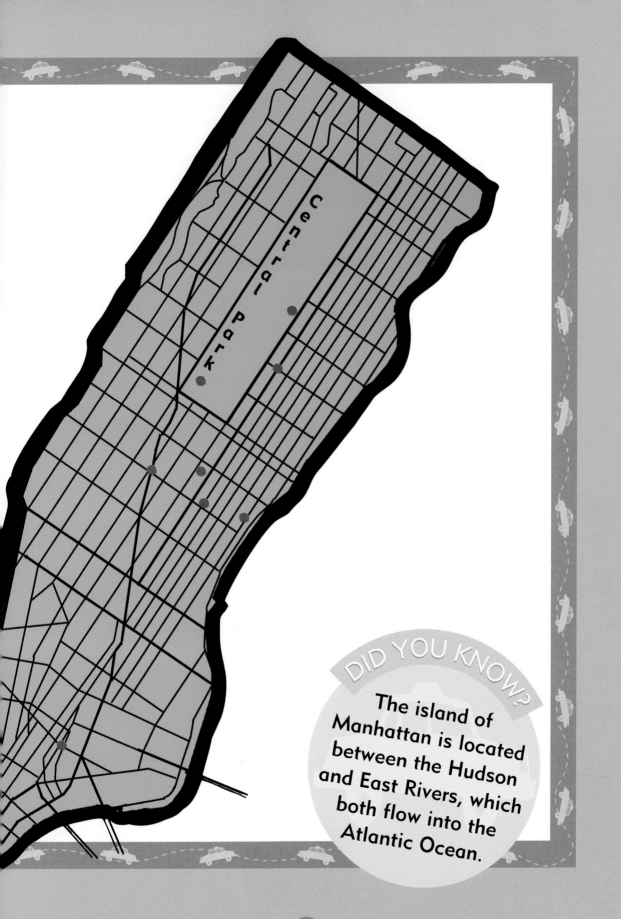

Central Park

The island of Manhattan is located between the Hudson and East Rivers, which both flow into the Atlantic Ocean.

GLOSSARY

A cabbie is also called a cabdriver. Cabbies drive cabs, short for taxicabs. Taxicabs are also called taxis.

A garage is an enclosed place where people can park automobiles and other vehicles. Taxicabs are parked in garages when they are not being driven.

A meter is a machine that keeps track of how much money passengers need to pay, based on how far they travel in a taxicab.

To hail a cab is to raise your arm high and wave, showing that you want a taxicab to stop for you. Sometimes people whistle or shout "Taxi!" when they want a cabbie to stop for them.

Tourists are people who visit someplace and who live somewhere else. Lots of tourists visit New York City because it's one of the most famous cities in the world.

A harbor is a place where boats and ships can dock and be protected from ocean weather. A ferry is a ship that travels short distances, from harbor to harbor.

Passengers are people who are traveling in a moving vehicle. You can be a passenger in an automobile, train, ferry, or airplane, for example.

Streetstands are common in New York City. They are places where you can buy food and drinks, and even things to wear, right on the sidewalk.

A popsicle is flavored ice on a stick. A pretzel is a twisted piece of dough that has been fried in oil and salted. A knish is baked or fried dough that is stuffed with potatoes or meat.

The books in the **Going Places** series
are produced by Orange Avenue, Inc.

Creative Director: **Hallie Warshaw**
Writer: **Robyn Brode** • Designer: **Britt Menendez**
Illustrator: **Paul Hayes** • Coordinator and
researcher: **Emily Vassos**
Photos: **Corbis, Eyewire,** and **Getty**

Original concept for series:
Hallie Warshaw and
Mark Shulman